Nigel the Narwhal

By
Joseph Pino

Artwork by
Dave Bogle

Nigel the Narwhal

Copyright © 2012 by Joseph Pino

Artwork by Dave Bogle

Author photo courtesy of author

The opinions expressed in this manuscript are solely the opinions of the author and do not represent the opinions or thoughts of the publisher. The author represents and warrants that s/he either owns or has the legal right to publish all material in this book.

ISBN-13: 9781519784544

First published in 2012

10 9 8 7 6 5 4 3 2 1

PRINTED IN THE UNITED STATES OF AMERICA

This book is dedicated to Connor and Emma.

Nigel the narwhal
loved to play.
He frolicked and jumped
all through the day.

As he grew up,

he started to find,

he wasn't quite like

the rest of his kind.

A horn started to grow,

right under his nose!

It didn't seem right;

it wasn't something he chose.

When Nigel was away,

his friends would chat,

they talked of his horn

and asked, "What's that?"

Embarrassed, Nigel quickly swam home for advice, hoping his parents' answer would suffice.

"Dear Father, come quick,

look what Nigel has grown,

a perfect little horn

to call his own!"

Father narwhal beamed
and took Nigel aside,
"Nigel, display your new horn high
and with pride."

"No other animal in the world
can lay claim,
to such a wondrous horn
steeped in fame."

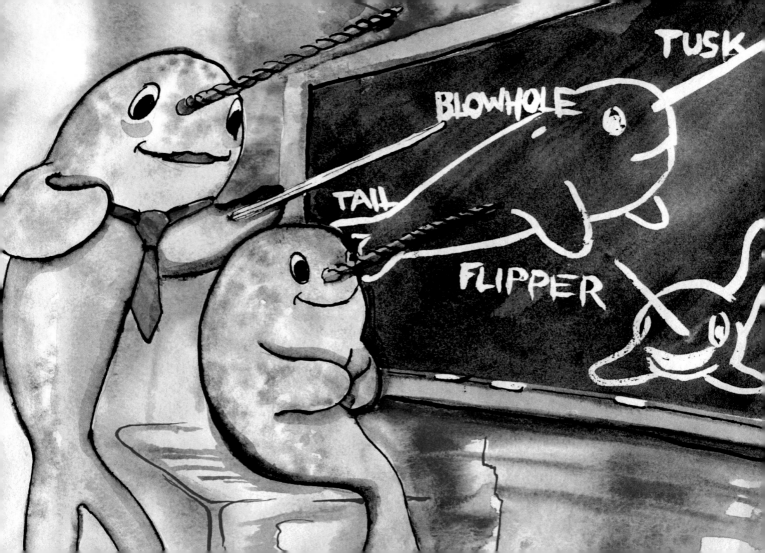

As Nigel sat and listened

to his father explain,

he began to understand

that his horn wasn't a pain!

It was unique to all whales
the entire worldwide,
he could play with his friends;
he didn't need to hide!

He went back to his friends,

and his story he told,

their understanding and acceptance

began to unfold.

Nigel and his friends
jumped and played,
shouts of laughter and joy
from their blowholes they sprayed.

Interesting Facts About Narwhals

- Nickname: unicorn of the sea
- Diet: fish, shrimp, squid
- Habitat: arctic waters
- Size: Newborn calf = 5 feet long

    Full grown = from 13 to 20 feet long
- Weight: Newborn calf = 175-220 pounds

    Full grown = can weigh up to 3,500 pounds
- The tusk is actually the left front tooth of the narwhal.
- The tusk/tooth can be up to 8 feet long.
- The tusk/tooth is normally found only in males; it is rare for a female narwhal to have a tusk (like Nigel's mom).
- Narwhals live together in family units called "pods" that can number up to 10-15 whales.

Source: http://animals.nationalgeographic.com/animals/mammals/narwhal/

Joseph Pino is the son of Italian immigrants who came to America in the early 1970s. He's had a lifelong fascination with whales, particularly the narwhal, ever since he learned about them in his sixth grade science class. Wanting to introduce these great animals to his own kids, he started looking for books on the subject. He soon discovered that there was a lack of children's books with whales as the subject. It was then that he created *Nigel the Narwhal*.

Joe currently lives in Michigan with his wife and their two children.

Made in the USA
San Bernardino, CA
26 April 2019